DATE DUE

The Fisherman's Son

adapted from a Georgian folktale

by **Mirra Ginsburg**
pictures by **Tony Chen**

GREENWILLOW BOOKS • New York

Published by Greenwillow Books
A Division of William Morrow
& Company, Inc.
105 Madison Avenue
New York, N.Y. 10016
Printed in
the United States of America
First Edition
10 9 8 7 6 5 4 3 2 1

Library of Congress Cataloging in Publication Data
Ginsburg, Mirra. The fisherman's son.
Summary: A fisherman's son saves the lives of four
animals who in turn help him accomplish the impossible
tasks set him by the woman he wants to marry.
[1. Folklore—Georgia (Transcaucasia)
2. Folklore—Russia] I. Chen, Tony. II. Title.
PZ8.1.G455Fi 398.2'2'094795 [E] 78-31852
ISBN 0-688-80216-8 ISBN 0-688-84216-X lib. bdg.

To Tolya—M. G.
To Pura—T. C.

One fine, sunny day a fisher-
man went fishing in the river. He took his little son
with him. They caught so many fish in their net
that their pail would not hold them all.
"Watch the fish," said the father to the boy.
"I'll go home and bring another pail."

The boy looked at the fish. They were big and small, silvery and gray and brown. And shining bright among them was a little red one.

"This fish is too pretty to die," he said, and threw her back into the water.

The fish pulled out one of her scales and gave it to the boy. "Keep this scale. If you ever need help, come to the river and call 'Little red fish! Little red fish!' and I will come at once to help you."

When the fisherman returned and saw that the little red fish was gone, he flew into a fit of anger.

"Get out of my sight!" he cried to his son. "You'll never grow up to be a fisherman. Go away, go away!"

And the boy went away. He walked and walked till he came to the woods, and there he saw a deer chased by a hunter. The hunter was just aiming at the deer, but the boy ran between them and saved the deer's life.

Before he bounded off, the deer plucked a hair from his hide and said, "Keep this hair. If you ever need help, come to the woods and call 'Deer! Deer!' and I will come at once to help you."

The fisherman's son went on until he came to an open field. He looked up and he saw a huge eagle just about to swoop down on a stork. The boy threw a stone at the eagle and saved the stork's life. The grateful stork pulled out a feather from his tail and said, "Keep this feather. If you ever need help, take out the feather and call 'Stork! Stork!' and I will come at once to help you."

The boy went on. Along the roadside he saw a pack of dogs chasing a fox. He drove away the dogs and saved the fox.

The grateful fox pulled out a whisker from his chin and said, "Keep this whisker. If you ever need help, come to the hills and call 'Fox! 'Fox!' and I will come at once to help you."

The fisherman's son went on and on, for weeks and months and years. He had many adventures and grew into a fine young man. One day he met a maiden. She was clever, beautiful, and rich, and he decided he must marry her.

This maiden owned a magic mirror that nobody could hide from. No matter how well you hid yourself, the mirror would find you and show you to its mistress. And the maiden had declared that she would never marry anyone except the man who hid himself so cleverly that the mirror could not find him.

"Well, now I need help," said the young man to himself. He went to the river, took out the scale of the fish and called, "Little red fish! Little red fish!" The little fish, who had by now grown into a big fish, appeared at once. The fisherman's son told her about his heart's desire, and the fish took him on her back and swam out quickly to the middle of the sea. She dove down to the very deepest spot, hid him behind a large rock, and shielded him from sight with her own body.

The maiden looked into the mirror and saw the young man at the bottom of the sea.
He came back and he said to her, "You'll never guess where I was."
And the maiden said, "I won't? The red fish took you to the bottom of the sea. She hid you behind a rock, and covered you from sight with her own body."
"Well, then, I'll try again," said the young man.

He went to the woods, took out the deer's hair and
called, "Deer! Deer!"
The deer appeared at once. The young man leaped up
on his back, and the deer carried him into the very
thick of the dense, trackless forest. He hid him in a
cave, and shielded him from sight with his own body.

The maiden looked into the mirror and saw the
fisherman's son in the cave.
He came back and he said to her, "This time
you will not guess where I was."

The maiden laughed. "Ha! The deer took you into the dark, dense forest. He hid you in a cave, and covered you from sight with his own body."

"Well, then, I must try a third time," said the young man.

He went into the field, took out the stork's feather and called, "Stork! Stork!"
The stork appeared at once. He told the fisherman's son to get up on his back, and the stork rose into the air. They flew and flew, until they reached the very edge of the sky. There the stork hid him in a cloud and shielded him from sight with his own body.

The maiden looked into the mirror and saw the
young man hiding at the edge of the sky.
He came back and he said to her, "This time you
surely won't guess where I was! I was in a place
that even your magic mirror could not show you."
But the maiden said, "Silly! The stork hid you in a
cloud at the very edge of the sky, and covered you
from sight with his own body."
And the young man said, "In that case, will you
let me try just one more time?"
And since the maiden really liked him, she agreed.

He went into the hills, took out the fox's whisker and called,
"Fox! Fox!"
The fox appeared at once. The fisherman's son told him about his
heart's desire, and the fox led him away and away, to a place
beyond nine mountains and eight deep valleys. There he began to
dig the earth with his paws. He dug and dug, until he had dug a
tunnel right to the cellar of the house where the
maiden lived. Then he brought the young
man into the house and hid him
under the maiden's own bed.

The maiden sat on her bed and looked into the
mirror and saw nothing but herself. She turned the
mirror to the mountains, to the woods, to the sky,
to the sea, but still she could not find the handsome
young man.
Then she cried out, "Where are you, sly one? Why
can't I see you anywhere?"

The fisherman's son came out of his hiding place,
and the maiden stared in amazement.
"You win," she said. "You are indeed a clever man.
And good, and handsome too. I'll marry you."

So they got married, and had a great wedding feast that lasted a whole year, and all their friends came to the wedding with precious gifts. The red fish brought a coral necklace for the bride. The deer brought a cradle inlaid with gold and silver. The stork came late, and brought a baby in a silken shawl. And the fox? The fox sat down by the cradle, and rocked the baby, and sang it songs and told it merry tales—about a fisherman's son, and a red fish, and a leaping deer, and a flying stork, and a sly fox who knew how to outwit a magic mirror.

DEC 1 0 1980